Heather Has Two Mommies

Lesléa Newman *illustrated by* Laura Cornell

CANDLEWICK PRESS

Heather lives in a little house with a big apple tree in the front yard and lots of tall grass in the backyard.

Heather's favorite number is two. She has two arms, two legs, two eyes, two ears, two hands, and two feet.

Heather has two pets:
a ginger-colored cat named Gingersnap
and a big black dog named Midnight.

Heather also has two mommies:
Mama Jane and Mama Kate.

Mama Kate is a doctor. She has two stethoscopes so she and Heather can listen to each other's heartbeats.

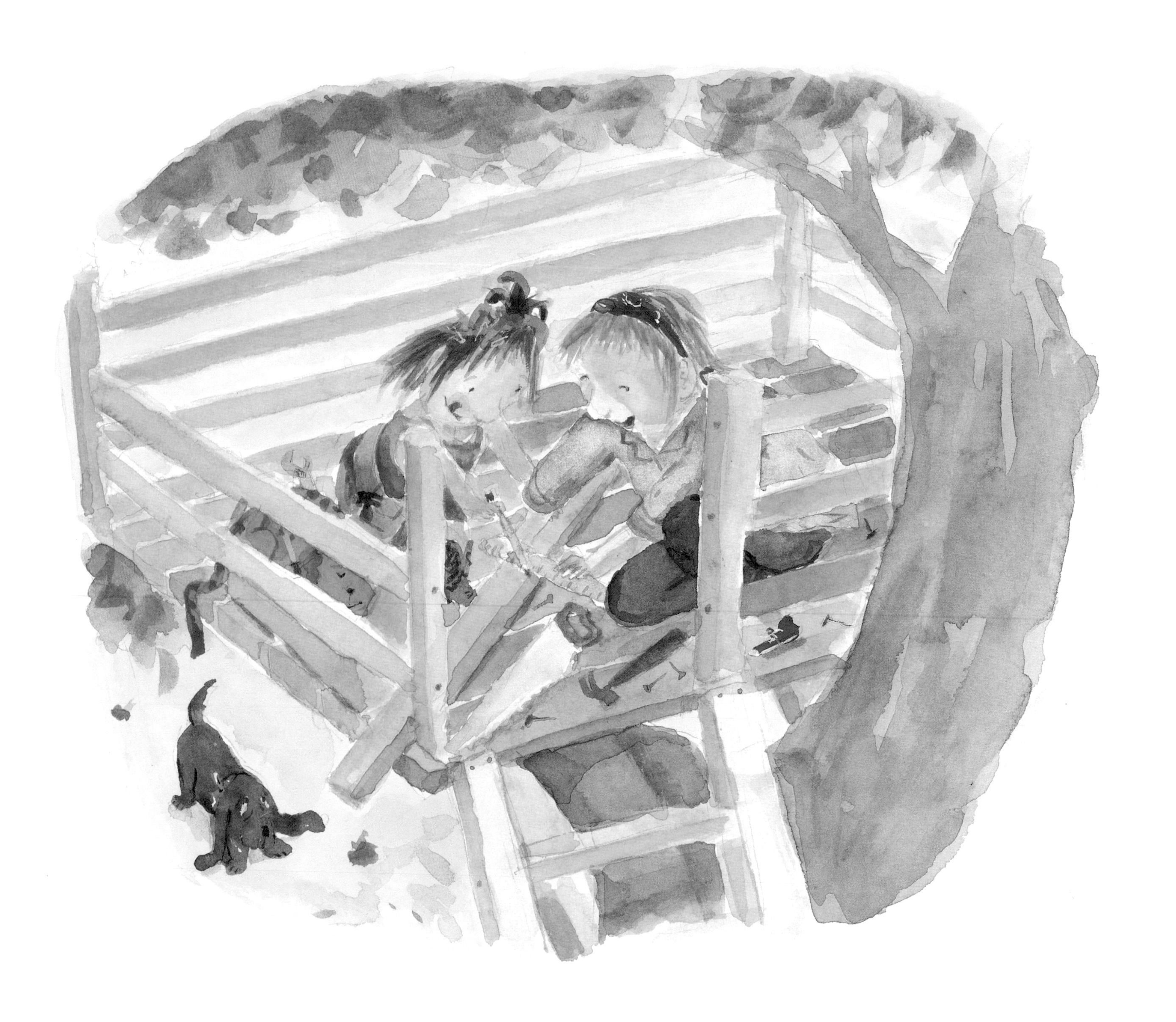

Mama Jane is a carpenter. She has two hammers so she and Heather can build things together.

Heather and her mommies have lots of fun together. On sunny days, they go to the park.

On rainy days, they stay inside and bake cookies. Heather likes to eat two gingersnaps and drink a big glass of milk.

One day, Mama Kate and Mama Jane tell Heather that they have a surprise for her. "You're going to start school next week!" Mama Kate says.

“There’ll be lots of other kids to play with and a teacher named Ms. Molly,” adds Mama Jane.

“Can Midnight and Gingersnap come, too?” asks Heather.

“No, they have to stay home,” Mama Jane says. “But you can bring two special things with you,” says Mama Kate.

Heather chooses her favorite blue blanket to rest with at nap time and her favorite red cup to drink out of at snack time.

Soon the big day arrives, and Mama Kate and Mama Jane take Heather to her new school.

There are so many things to play with! Heather sees building blocks, dress-up clothes, crayons, and paint. Heather also sees a big round table for snack time and a quiet cozy corner for nap time.

While Mama Jane and Mama Kate talk to Ms. Molly, Heather puts two puzzles together all by herself.

Soon it's time for Mama Jane and Mama Kate to leave. They kiss Heather good-bye, and Heather cries. But only a little.

leaves
collect rocks
ELEPHANTS at PLAY
INCLUDES: Several Pieces

Heather has lots of fun at her new school. She builds a tower out of building blocks . . .

and dresses up like a firefighter.

She drinks apple juice out of her favorite red cup at snack time and rests in the quiet corner with her favorite blue blanket at nap time.

After nap time, all the children sit in a circle while Ms. Molly reads them a story about a boy whose father is a veterinarian.

"Who knows what a veterinarian is?" asks Ms. Molly.

"I do! My mommy is a veterinarian," Juan says. "A veterinarian is an animal doctor."

"My daddy is a people doctor!" shouts David.

"My mommy is a people doctor, too!" Heather shouts even louder.

"What does your daddy do?" David asks Heather.

"I don't have a daddy," Heather says. She looks around the circle and wonders, *Am I the only one here who doesn't have a daddy?*

"I have an idea," Ms. Molly says. "Let's all draw pictures of our families."

Juan draws his mommy, daddy, and big brother, Carlos.

Miriam draws her mommy and her sister, Rachel, playing in the park.

Stacy draws her daddy and her papa
reading her stories.

Joshua hangs up the picture he drew of his mommy and stepfather dropping him off at his daddy's house.

Emily tapes up the picture she drew of her grandma and their two puppies, Emmet and Charlie.

David straightens out the picture he drew of the day his mommy and daddy brought his new sister, Veronica, home.

Ms. Molly looks at all the pictures. “It doesn’t matter how many mommies or how many daddies your family has,” Ms. Molly says. “It doesn’t matter if your family has sisters or brothers or cousins or grandmas or grandpas or uncles or aunts.”

"Each family is special. The most important thing about a family is that all the people in it love each other."

Soon Heather's first day of school is over. When Mama Kate and Mama Jane arrive to pick her up, Heather shows them all the pictures.

"Is that me?" Mama Kate asks, pointing to Heather's picture.

"And is that me?" Mama Jane asks, pointing, too.

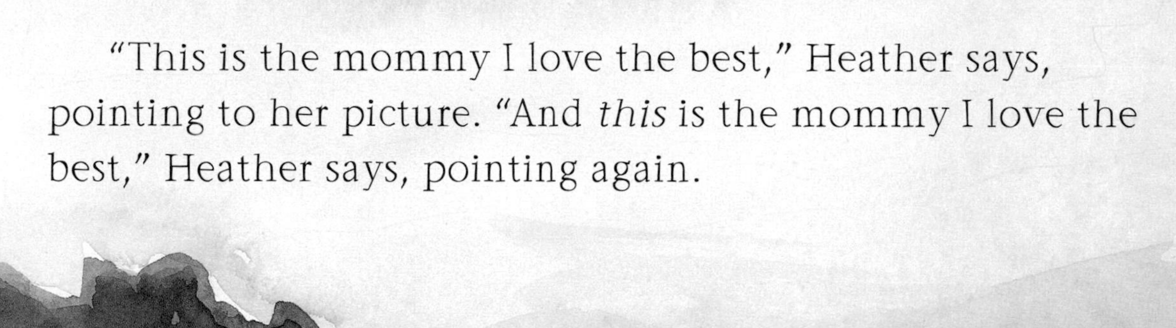

“This is the mommy I love the best,” Heather says, pointing to her picture. “And *this* is the mommy I love the best,” Heather says, pointing again.

Mama Kate and Mama Jane both laugh as Heather gives each of them two kisses. Then she takes their hands and they all head home.